Nate The Great
and The
Boring Beach Bag

Nate The Great
and The
Boring Beach Bag

by Marjorie Weinman Sharmat

illustrated by Marc Simont

A Yearling Book

Published by
Bantam Doubleday Dell Books for Young Readers
a division of
Bantam Doubleday Dell Publishing Group, Inc.
1540 Broadway
New York, New York 10036

ISBN: 0-440-40168-2

Reprinted by arrangement with The Putnam & Grossett Group

Printed in the United States of America

June 1989

25 24 23 22 21

UPR

To the beach of my childhood,
Old Orchard Beach, Maine

I, Nate, the great detective,
was swimming in the ocean
with my dog, Sludge.

7

Someone was swimming behind us.

It was Oliver.

Oliver is always behind me.

Oliver is a pest.

He swam up beside me.

"I lost my seashell,"

he said. "I want you to find it."

"I, Nate the Great,

do not look for seashells.

If I did, I could find plenty
of them on this beach."

"The seashell was in my beach bag,"
Oliver said. "But that is gone, too."

"Your beach bag is gone?"

"Yes," Oliver said. "My clothes
and shoes were in it."

"Your clothes and shoes, too?
You need clothes.
You need shoes.
You need me.

I, Nate the Great,

will take your case."

Sludge, Oliver and I swam to shore.

We sat down on the sand.

I took a pencil and a piece of paper
out of my swimsuit pocket.
I wrote a note to my mother.
It was soggy and sandy.
I hoped she could read it.

11

Dear mother,
I am on a soggy
and sandy case.
I will be back.
I might be back
before you get this note.
I am sending it with
Sludge.
Love
Nate the Great

I put the note in Sludge's mouth.
"Take this home
and then come back," I said.
"Don't stop to eat
along the way."
Sludge ran off with the note.
I hoped he would be back soon.

I hoped he would be back.

Oliver and I walked along the beach.

"Show me where you last saw

your beach bag," I said.

"I left it on the beach,"

Oliver said, "while I bought

a glass of water

at Rosamond's Restaurant."

"Rosamond has a restaurant?"

"Yes. She is selling water,

seaweed soup, and sandwiches.

The sandwiches are filled with sand.

She said that

since they are called sandwiches,

they should be made of sand."

"It figures," I said.

Oliver stopped.

"When I got back
to where I left my beach bag,
it was gone. And here is where
I left it."

"How do you know that?" I asked.

"Because I left my beach ball

beside it. And see, my beach ball
is still here. Nobody took it."
"If somebody took your beach bag,
why would they leave your beach ball?"
I asked. "Was there something special
about your beach bag?
What did it look like?"
"It was blue.
It was blank.
It was boring,"
Oliver said.
"And it was bumpy
from all the stuff inside it."
I, Nate the Great, looked down
at the beach ball
and the sand around it.

"The sand is not pressed down
where your beach bag was," I said,
"even though the bag was heavy
with clothes, shoes,
and a shell inside it."
"Is that a clue?" Oliver asked.
"It may be an important clue
or no clue at all," I said.
"Sand gets kicked around.
Tell me, were you alone when
you left your beach bag here?"

"I was sitting all by myself,"
Oliver said. "Then I saw
Annie and her dog, Fang,
running toward me.
Whenever I see Fang
running toward me,
I run, too.
I run away.
I ran to Rosamond's Restaurant."
"We will have to walk to
Rosamond's Restaurant," I said.

"We will look for clues
and your boring beach bag
along the way."
Oliver and I started to walk.
The sun felt hot
on my back.

18

The sand felt scratchy

between my toes.

I was careful not to step

on sand castles

or ice cream sticks.

I ducked beach balls in the air.

I looked for Oliver's beach bag.

I also looked for Sludge.

He should have been back by now.

We passed a refreshment stand.

I wondered if they served pancakes.

I wanted to stop.

But I had a case to solve.

I saw Rosamond up ahead.

She was sitting behind a crate.

Sometimes people get strange

sitting under a hot sun.

But Rosamond is strange all the time.

Rosamond's four cats were asleep
on the crate.

Oliver and I walked up to her.

"Have you seen Oliver's
boring beach bag?" I asked.

"No," Rosamond said. "I have been
too busy with my restaurant.
Want to buy a sandwich or soup
or a glass of water?"

"No. I must find the beach bag.
Oliver has no clothes, no shoes,
and no seashell."

"Oh, dear," Rosamond said.
"I will give him some free water.
And part of a sandwich."

Rosamond handed Oliver
a glass of sandy water.

I knew it was time to leave.

Oliver and I started to walk back
to where he said he had left
his beach bag.

"I did not find your beach bag
between where you left it
and Rosamond's Restaurant," I said.
"I also did not find my dog."
I, Nate the Great, was thinking.
Sludge must have stopped somewhere
to eat.
That sounded like a good idea.
"I am going to stop
at the refreshment stand," I said.
I walked up to the refreshment stand.
Oliver followed me.
Then he stopped.
Suddenly I knew why.
Annie's dog, Fang, was tied
to a post beside the stand.

His teeth gleamed
under the bright sun.
He looked hungry.
He looked at me.
I did not want to stay.
But Annie was there.
Perhaps she had seen Oliver's bag.
I talked fast.
"I am looking for Oliver's
beach bag," I said.
"It looks boring.
Have you seen it?"

"Yes, it was beside
a beach ball," Annie said.
"Fang and I ran by it,
just as Oliver ran off.
Fang and I are running
from one end of the beach
to the other.

I stopped for a snack.

But Fang is trying to lose weight.

He is on a diet."

"He is eating the post

you tied him to," I said.

"But that is not on his diet!"

Annie cried.

She rushed to Fang

and untied him.

"Is a beach bag on his diet?"

I asked.

"Not today," Annie said.

Annie and Fang ran off.

They ran in the opposite direction

from Rosamond's Restaurant.

Fang was not so hungry

that he would eat a sandwich

made of sand.

I, Nate the Great, was hungry.

I ate some pancakes

at the refreshment stand

and thought about the case.

There was not much to think about.

I did not have one clue

that I knew was a clue.

I also did not have a dog.

Where was Sludge?

Suddenly I saw him on the beach.

He was with Oliver.

I finished my pancakes fast.

I went up to Sludge and Oliver.

Sludge was still holding my note
in his mouth.

He looked hot and tired.

"You were supposed to take
that note home," I said.
Perhaps Sludge did not know
where home was.
The beach looks the same
for miles and miles.
Sand and water.
All that sand
and all that water

must have mixed him up.
Sludge sat down and rested.
Oliver and I sat with him.
Then Sludge ran into the water
to cool off.
The *water*.
I had been looking for Oliver's
beach bag on land.
But what if it was in the water?

I ran into the water.

I swam here.

I swam there.

I looked and looked

for Oliver's beach bag.

All of a sudden I saw it!

It was bobbing in the water

up ahead.

A bump.

A big blue bump.

Sludge and I swam up to it.

I grabbed it.

It was not Oliver's beach bag.

It was Esmeralda's head.

"What are you doing?" she asked.

"I am looking for Oliver's

beach bag," I said.

"Oliver!" cried Esmeralda.

"I am hiding from him.

He follows me everywhere.

On land.

On sea.

And here he comes!"

Esmeralda swam away.

33

Oliver swam up.

"Did you find my beach bag?"

he asked.

"Not yet," I said.

"I will follow you

until you solve the case,"

Oliver said.

"And even after I solve the case,"

I said.

Sludge and I swam to shore.

Oliver swam to shore.
Sludge and I stretched out
on the sand.
Oliver stretched out
on the sand behind us.
He had given me a tough case.
Nobody had given me any clues.

Or had they?
There was no dent in the sand
from Oliver's beach bag.
What if it meant something?
What if it meant that
Oliver's beach bag
had *never* been there?
But Oliver said it had.
What else did he say?
He said that Annie and Fang
were running toward him
just before he left
his beach bag and beach ball

and ran to Rosamond's Restaurant.

I, Nate the Great, got a stick.

I smoothed out some sand.

Then I drew a map in it.

I marked where Oliver's beach ball was.

I marked Rosamond's Restaurant.

I marked the refreshment stand,

which was between them.

I had seen Annie and Fang

at the refreshment stand.

Annie said that they were running

from one end of the beach

to the other.

She said they had run past
Oliver's beach bag and ball.
I looked at my map.
First there was the beach ball.
Then the refreshment stand.
Then Rosamond's Restaurant.
When Annie and Fang left
the refreshment stand,
they should have run
toward Rosamond's Restaurant.
But they ran in the opposite direction.
Why?
I, Nate the Great, was stumped.
I looked at Sludge.
Sludge always helps with my cases.
But all the sand and water

had mixed him up this time.

Did Annie and Fang get mixed up?

No. Annie would not

get mixed up.

I looked at Oliver.

It would be easy

for him to get mixed up.

He was always following someone.

I kicked some sand.

I ducked a beach ball.

I thought.

Hmm.

"Oliver," I said.

"I think I know

where your beach bag is.

Follow me."

"Of course," Oliver said.

Sludge and I walked
to Rosamond's Restaurant.
We walked *past* Rosamond's Restaurant.
"Wait!" Oliver said.
"You are going very far away
from where I left my beach bag."
I, Nate the Great, kept on walking.
Up ahead I saw something in the sand.

ROSAMOND'S RESTAURANT
Cold WATER 3¢ A GLASS
SEAWEED Soup   A PICKLE
SANDWICHES ALL SAND
NO FAKE 4 CENTS

I ran up to it.

It was a beach bag.

It was blue.

It was blank.

It was bumpy.

It was boring.

It was Oliver's beach bag.

"My beach bag!" Oliver cried.

"What is it doing *here*?"

"It was *always* here," I said.

"No one took it.

But someone took your *beach ball*.

Someone picked it up and threw it.

Or kicked it. Or carried it.

And I think it got thrown or kicked

again and again.

It landed a long way

from where you left it.

The sand was not pressed down

next to where you found

your beach ball

because your beach bag

had never been there.

But Annie gave me the big clue.

She and Fang are running

from one end of the beach

to the other.

I saw them run

toward the place

where you said you had left

your beach bag and ball.

But she had already *seen*

your ball and bag.

How could she see them

when she had not yet reached the place

where you said you had left them?

She or you had to be wrong."

"So you picked me?" Oliver asked.

"Yes, I, Nate the Great, picked you.

After someone almost hit me

on the head
with a beach ball.
That is when I thought
that the ball, not the bag,
had moved.
You left your beach bag
and beach ball *here*.
You went to Rosamond's Restaurant
over there. Then what did you do?"
"I drank my glass of water
and followed Esmeralda," Oliver said.
"When I saw my beach ball, I stopped."
"I, Nate the Great, say that
you followed Esmeralda *away* from
where you left your bag and ball.
When you saw your ball

you thought you were back
at where you had left it.
It is easy to get mixed up
on the beach.
If you are following someone,
it is even easier.
The case is solved."

"I will never follow anyone
again," Oliver said.

"Good," I said. "Sludge and I
are going for a swim."
"I just changed my mind,"
Oliver said.
"I knew it," I said.
I, Nate the Great,
and Sludge,
and Oliver, of course,
dove into the water.